THE CASE OF THE
WET BED

For Kate, whose love and strength touched everyone around her—HJB

For my family, both then and now—SG

THE CASE OF THE
WET BED

by Howard J. Bennett, MD

illustrated by Spike Gerrell

MAGINATION PRESS
WASHINGTON, DC
American Psychological Association

Published by
MAGINATION PRESS
An Educational Publishing Foundation Book
American Psychological Association
750 First Street, NE
Washington, DC 20002

For more information about our books, including a complete catalog, please write to us,
call 1-800-374-2721, or visit our website at www.apa.org/pubs/magination.

Book design by Susan White
Printed by Worzalla, Stevens Point, Wisconsin

Library of Congress Cataloging-in-Publication Data
Bennett, Howard J.
Max Archer, kid detective : the case of the wet bed / by Howard J. Bennett ;
illustrated by Spike Gerrell.
p. cm.
ISBN-13: 978-1-4338-0953-8 (hardcover : alk. paper)
ISBN-10: 1-4338-0953-2 (hardcover : alk. paper)
ISBN-13: 978-1-4338-0954-5 (pbk. : alk. paper)
ISBN-10: 1-4338-0954-0 (pbk. : alk. paper)
1. Enuresis—Juvenile literature. 2. Enuresis—Psychological aspects—Juvenile literature.
I. Gerrell, Spike, ill. II. Title.

RJ476.E6B459 2011
618.92'849--dc22   2010051485

Contents

CHAPTER 1   Call Me Max 7

CHAPTER 2   I'll Be Right Over 11

CHAPTER 3   The Pee, the Whole Pee,
and Nothing But the Pee...............15

CHAPTER 4   Poop Patrol..................................19

CHAPTER 5   The Stream Team.......................24

CHAPTER 6   Message to Brain:
Get Up and GO 31

CHAPTER 7   All's Well That Ends Well..............39

Extra Activities and Information 41

Q&A About Bedwetting (Just for Parents!)...............46

CHAPTER 1

Call Me Max

My name is Max.
Max Archer.
I'm a kid detective.
That means I help kids
with their problems.

Because you're reading this, I'm assuming you wet the bed. Maybe not every night, but enough that someone bought the book for you.

I wet the bed when I was a kid, too. For years.
I didn't mind being wet when I was little because I slept in diapers. But when I turned five, it started to bother me.

I was sick of waking up smelling like pee.

I was afraid to go on sleepovers.

But worst of all, my 3-year-old sister was dry at night.

My mom never made me feel bad about wetting the bed, but I could tell she was tired of washing my stinky sheets.

One day, I overheard my parents talking.

"I think Max could be dry if he just put his mind to it," said Dad.

"I'm not so sure," said Mom.

"Then how come he can be dry for three days in a row and then wet the bed again?"

"I don't know," said Mom. "But the doctor told me that kids don't always wake up when they have to go. She said that no one wets the bed on purpose."

The doctor also said I would outgrow the problem and shouldn't worry about it.

I did outgrow my bedwetting, but not until I was eleven years old!

That's when I decided to become a kid detective.
If doctors could not solve a kid's problems, somebody had to. And I guess that somebody was me.

I still had to go to school and stuff. But once my homework and chores were done, my office door was always open.

CHAPTER 2

I'll Be Right Over

I was in my office reading *Calvin and Hobbes* when I got a call from Billy Parker. Billy was eight. He had just been to the doctor for a checkup. The doctor said he was very healthy. When Billy mentioned that he wet the bed, the doctor told him not to worry because he would outgrow the problem.

Billy got in touch with me because he didn't want to wait forever to become dry, and his parents reminded him that I had helped one of the Miller twins who lived around the corner.

I told Billy I was free until five o'clock, when I had a soccer game.

"I can be at your house in fifteen minutes," he said.

"Great," I said. "Come on over."

When Billy arrived, I asked him if he wanted a glass of OJ or a cup of hot chocolate. He chose the hot chocolate.

The first thing I told Billy was that LOTS of kids wet the bed.

"Billy, there are five million kids in the United States that go to bed every night not knowing if they will wake up wet or dry."

"Really?" said Billy.

"Really," I said. "Do you know how big the number five million is?"

"No," said Billy sheepishly.

I gave him a few examples so he could understand what we were talking about.

- If five million elephants were lined up end to end, they would stretch all the way around the world.

- If five million children went to a professional baseball game, you would need 100 stadiums to find them all seats.

- If you had five million M&Ms, you could fill up a backyard swimming pool. (Unless my dad was nearby— he loves M&Ms.)

"Wow!" said Billy. "There really are lots of kids who wet the bed."

"That's right," I said. "But most kids are too embarrassed to talk about it."

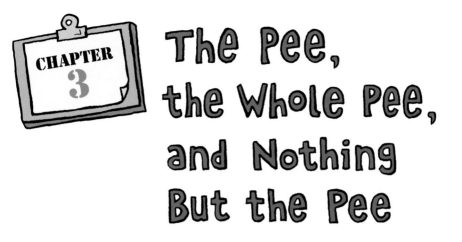

CHAPTER 3

The Pee, the Whole Pee, and Nothing But the Pee

Once I helped Billy understand that lots of kids wet the bed, I showed him where pee comes from and how the body gets rid of it.

MaX ARCHeR PReSeNTS

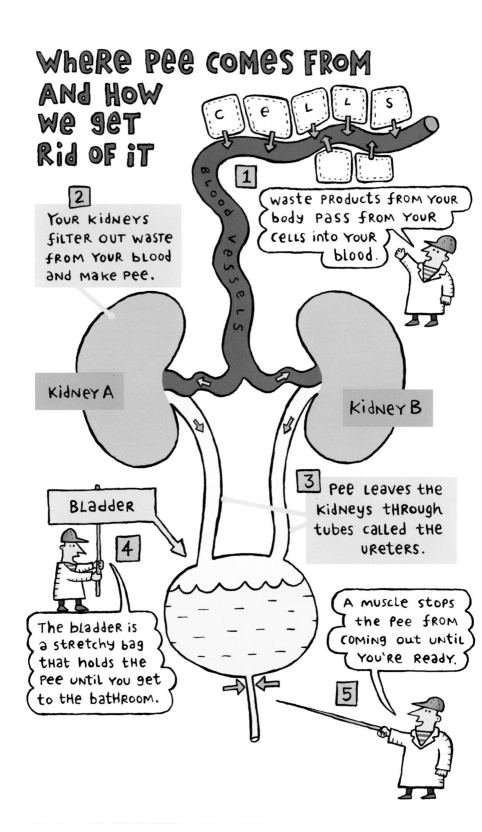

"Here's the way it works, Billy. Each of the cells in your body is like a tiny machine. And just like a car produces exhaust that comes out of its tail pipe, your cells make waste products that need to get out of your body."

"How?" said Billy.

"First, the waste passes from your cells into your blood. Then the blood travels to your kidneys, which are like big filters that remove the waste and make pee."

"Is that why pee smells bad?" asked Billy.

"You bet. Pee contains ammonia, which is very smelly. Ammonia is also a good cleaning agent, which is why the ancient Romans used pee to brush their teeth."

"Gross!" said Billy.

"Pee gets out of the body by traveling from your kidneys to your bladder. The bladder is a muscular pouch that's sort of like a balloon. It holds your pee until you can get to the bathroom. If you didn't have a bladder, pee would constantly drip out of your body like a leaky faucet."

"Double gross!" said Billy.

"Tell me about it! The reason you know it's time to pee is because the bladder sends a message to your brain when it fills up. Some people feel a tickle when they get this message. Others feel pressure or a mild ache."

"I get a tickle when I need to pee," said Billy.

"Me too," I said.

CHAPTER 4

POOP PATROL

We were making progress faster than you can say double cheeseburger with a side order of fries. Billy was a smart kid and a quick learner. He was ready for the next step.

"The reason most kids wet the bed is because their brain doesn't pay attention to their bladder when they're sleeping," I said.

"Then how can I become dry at night?" said Billy.

"By learning to pay attention to your bladder when you're awake and by doing some exercises before you go to sleep at night."

"Can I start right away?" said Billy.

"Not yet," I said. "First we need to do some detective work."

"What kind of detective work?"

"For one thing, we need to find out about your poops, because kids can wet the bed if they don't poop often enough or if they have really big poops."

"How does poop affect the bladder?" said Billy.

"Look at this picture that shows a side view of your body. Right behind the bladder is something called the rectum. This is where your poop sits before it leaves your body."

"I didn't know poop could sit," said Billy. "Can it stand and do cartwheels, too?"

"Very funny," I said. "If a person has lots of poop in his rectum, it can push on the bladder. That makes it harder for the bladder to hold your pee, especially at night."

"I see," said Billy. "And if my rectum is filled with less poop, my bladder would do a better job holding my pee."

"Exactly."

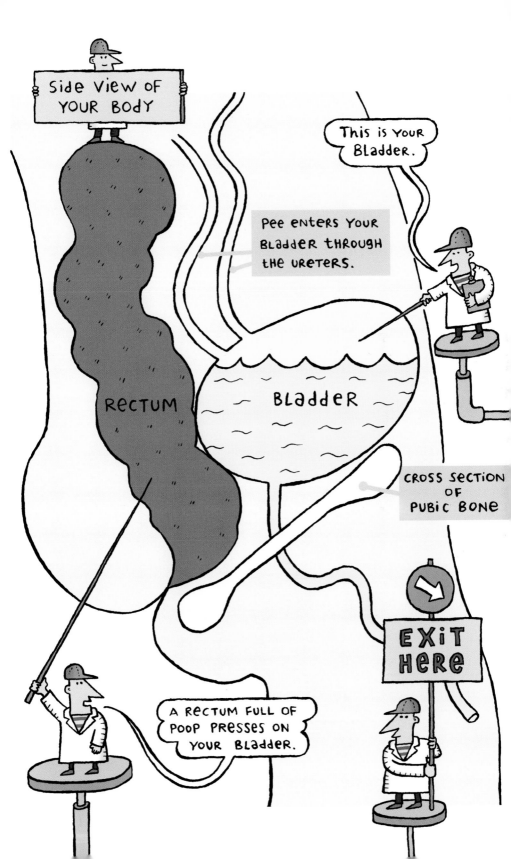

"How does this involve detective work?" said Billy.

"Most people don't know how often they poop or what their poop looks like. So you need to go on Poop Patrol," I said.

"What's that?" said Billy.

"For the next week, work with your parents to keep a record of all of your poops—what they look like and how often they come out. Just tell your mom and dad that you're joining the Poop Police! You can even make them your deputies."

"Cool," said Billy. "Do I get to wear a badge?"

"Sure. And if you're not having soft, easy-to-pass poops every day, eat more fruits and veggies. Plus, have a look at this this pamphlet I wrote: *How to Become a Super Duper Pooper.*"

"Catchy title," said Billy.

"Thanks," I said.

CHAPTER 5

The Stream Team

Billy left my office ready to go on Poop Patrol. He was feeling good about this new plan. He came back to see me two weeks later. Billy brought his poop record, which was a good sign that he was really motivated to work on becoming dry at night.

"How'd it go?" I said, after Billy sat down and took a sip of hot chocolate. (I always remember what my clients like to drink.)

"I asked my mom to help, and we figured out that I was having big poops every three or four days. I followed the suggestions in your pamphlet and now I'm having a soft poop every day. But I'm still wet at night."

"That's okay," I said. "You've taken the first step, and I don't expect you to have dry nights right away. Besides, we have to add a few more steps to the program."

"Like what?" said Billy.

see page 42-43

How to become a Super Duper Pooper

by Max Archer

24

"We need you to pay more attention to your bladder and to have more practice peeing during the day."

"But I hate going to the bathroom," said Billy.

"Lots of kids feel the same way you do. Either they don't want to stop what they're doing to pee or they get grossed out because the bathroom at school smells so bad."

"How'd you know?"

"Dude, why do you think I'm the best kid detective in town? I know my stuff."

"Right. I forgot," said Billy.

"Okay, the next part is pretty easy. You basically need to make sure you drink a glass of milk or juice at breakfast and lunch. You also need to drink something when you come home from school. This will make you pee more, which will help you understand how your bladder sends messages to your brain when it needs to go."

"Okay," said Billy. "I'll ask my mom to give me juice at breakfast and I'll get a glass of water when I come home from school."

"I already drink a glass of milk at lunch every day. What about after dinner? Can I have something to drink then?"

"Of course," said Max. "My mom asked me not to drink anything after dinner when I was your age because she thought it would help me stay dry. It didn't work, so I never suggest this to my clients."

"Gotcha," said Billy.

"Perfect," I said. "The next step is to pay more attention to your bladder. Whenever you get the urge to pee, stop what you're doing and go to the bathroom right away. On the way to the bathroom, concentrate on the feeling that's letting you know it's time to go. If you pay attention to this feeling during the day, it will help you become dry at night."

"I can do that," said Billy.

"I knew you could. You are now a member of the Stream Team."

Message to Brain: Get up and Go

Now that Billy had learned to pay attention to his bladder, he was a member of the Stream Team.

"Is that all I need to do?" said Billy.

"No," I said. "There are two more steps. The first one is called Waking Up Practice."

"What's that?" said Billy.

"You pee right before you go to sleep at night don't you?"

"Of course," said Billy.

"Good. Only now I don't want you to go to the bathroom the way you normally do. Instead, I want you to lie down in bed with the lights out and do the following steps:

1. Pretend it's the middle of the night and your bladder is sending a message to your brain telling you it's time to go.

2. Imagine your bladder is filling up with pee and sending a strong message for you to wake up.

3. Get out of bed, walk to the bathroom, and pee into the toilet."

"I get it," said Billy. "You want me to practice what I'll need to do if my bladder can't hold all of my pee until morning."

"Bingo!" I said.

It's easier to get up at night if you have a nightlight in your room.

"But what if my bladder can hold all of my pee until morning?"

"That would be great!" I said. "In fact, you have figured out the next part of the program. After you finish your Waking Up Practice, I want you to get in bed and give yourself one more message before you go to sleep. The message can be in your own words, but it should go something like this: If I need to go at night, my bladder will hold all of my pee until morning. But if it can't hold all of my pee, I will wake up by myself and go to the bathroom. Repeat the message a few times before you go to sleep."

"Sweet!" said Billy. "I will imagine my bladder filling up with pee when I give myself the message."

If I need to go at night
My bladder will hold all of my PEE
Till Morning
But if I can't hold all of my PEE I will
wake myself up and go to the bathroom

cat

"Great idea. Just one more step and you're on your way."

"Let's have it," said Billy enthusiastically.

"It's important to keep track of your wet and dry nights so you can see the progress you're making. So I want you to keep a calendar to record what happens at night. There are three ways to mark the calendar.

If you have a dry night, write D on the calendar.

If your underpants are wet but the sheets are dry, write SW (small wet) on the calendar.

If your underpants and sheets get wet, write LW (large wet) on the calendar.

Your deputies can help you remember to fill out the calendar in case you forget."

Night Time Record

	week 1	week 2	week 3	week 4
M				
T				
W				
Th				
F				
Sa				
Su				

KEY: **D** = Dry Night
SW = small wet
LW = Large wet

"Got it," said Billy. "How soon can I expect to have dry nights?"

"That varies from person to person," I said. "Some kids start having dry nights fairly soon. For others it takes longer. A positive attitude is important, as is lots of support from your mom and dad."

"Sounds great," said Billy. "I'm confident your program will help. When do you want to see me again?"

"Call me or send me an email in a couple of weeks so I know how you're doing."

"Will do," said Billy. "Wish me luck."

"Good luck," I said as Billy left to go home. He was so excited about the program that he forgot to finish his hot chocolate.

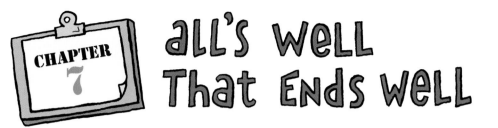

all's well That ends well

I got an email from Billy four weeks later. This is what it said—

Hi Max,

Your program is awesome! Before I saw you,
I was wet almost every night. Now I'm dry
three or four nights a week. I know it may
take a while to become completely dry, but
I'm on my way.

Billy
P.S. I went on my first sleepover the other
night. I had a great time, and I woke up dry!

I hit the reply button and sent Billy the following email—

Hi Billy,

That's great news, but I'm not surprised you're doing so well. Let me know if you don't become completely dry in the next six months. I have another program that takes more work, but it can help even more. It involves using a device called the bedwetting alarm.

Max, Kid Detective
P.S. You're a great kid!

extra activities and information

How to Become A SuPeR DuPeR PooPeR ⭐ by Max ⭐

This may sound funny, but most kids do not think about pooping. Basically, you feel the urge to go, you find a bathroom, you poop. (If you were hiking in the woods when this happened, you might find a tree instead!) Many people poop every day. Others go two or three times a week. There is nothing wrong with going a couple of times per week unless it causes stomachaches or makes it harder for your bladder to hold your pee at night.

But where does poop come from? Poop is the waste that is left over after you have digested your food. When you eat, food passes from your mouth to your stomach and small intestine ⇨ where most of the digestion takes place. Your body uses chemicals and lots of water to break down food particles into tiny molecules that can be absorbed into your bloodstream. These particles are dissolved in your blood and travel to all the cells in your body. Without this process, you wouldn't have enough nutrients and energy to grow, think, or bug your sister.

Once food is digested, a gooey, watery waste is left over. This is the stuff that enters your large intestine. The large intestine is only five feet long, but it has an important job to do. Because you use so much water to digest food, you would become dehydrated if the water wasn't reabsorbed before leaving your body. That is the job of the large intestine.

As the liquid waste makes its journey through the large intestine, more and more water is removed. During this process, it becomes firmer and it turns into solid waste. (The grownup word for poop is feces.) If the waste moves through your large intestine slowly, ↳

more water is reabsorbed, resulting in harder poops. If the waste moves through your large intestine quickly, less water is reabsorbed, resulting in softer poops.

What To Do If You Have Big or Hard Poops

Drink plenty of liquids during the day and eat lots of roughage. (That's the fancy word for some of the healthy stuff that's in fruits, vegetables, and whole grain bread and pasta.) The reason this works is because liquids and roughage speed up how quickly poop moves through the large intestine.

Exercise also helps, but not getting enough exercise is more of a problem for grownups than kids.

Pay attention to your body. Lots of kids hold in their poops if they feel the urge to go when they are busy reading, playing, or goofing around on the computer. If you squeeze your butt muscles to keep your poop inside, it will make the urge go away, but only for a little while. In the end—no pun intended—the poop will become bigger and harder to pass. So if your body says it's time to go, stop what you're doing and GO!

Practice pooping. Sit on the toilet for five minutes twice a day even if you DON'T feel the urge to go. By sitting on the toilet, you give your body a chance to let the poop out. The best time to do this is ten or fifteen minutes after you eat. Some kids like to use a timer to let them know when Pooping Practice is over. It is no big deal if you do not poop. Just try again later.

Keep a Poop Chart so you know how often you go. Put the information on a card or small piece of paper that is kept in the bathroom.

WoRd seaRch

Some foods make your poops bigger and harder to come out. Other foods make your poops softer and easier to come out. Eat more of the foods that make poops soft, and that will help your bladder do its job, too.

Find food words that will make poops soft!

raisins	broccoli	peas	carrots	green beans
lettuce	spinach	pears	watermelon	grapes
peaches	oranges	prunes	water	juice

```
D  I  T  Q  I  F  V  P  P  E  C  I  U  J  X
P  G  T  Q  V  N  R  E  S  N  I  S  I  A  R
E  Q  R  P  I  U  O  S  P  I  N  A  C  H  J
A  H  E  E  N  J  D  L  D  D  H  T  Z  X  F
C  V  X  E  E  H  X  T  E  H  K  N  A  S  M
H  T  S  K  R  N  H  S  A  M  P  Y  E  O  P
E  Z  B  P  W  A  B  M  R  P  R  P  V  E  R
S  Z  B  A  Q  C  T  E  I  A  A  E  A  D  Z
L  E  T  T  U  C  E  P  A  R  E  S  T  G  V
V  E  X  U  D  L  N  M  G  N  G  P  P  A  L
R  U  O  R  A  N  G  E  S  F  S  M  D  F  W
C  A  R  R  O  T  S  W  U  T  U  B  X  I  U
T  M  W  H  Q  Y  Z  K  A  N  I  P  Z  Z  K
W  R  I  L  R  F  F  U  P  M  T  A  Z  T  L
B  H  K  Q  Y  M  B  R  O  C  C  O  L  I  J
```

Make your own badges

Your Name

KID
DETECTIVE

Paste your photo here

Poop Patrol

Stream Team

Deputy

Q&A ABOUT BEDWETTING
(JUST FOR PARENTS!)

Bedwetting is a common condition that affects about five million children in the United States. Still, parents have lots of questions. Here are some:

Q *Does bedwetting run in families?*

A Most children who wet the bed have at least one parent or another close relative who had the same problem as a child. This is good to know for two reasons. First, parents can feel reassured that nothing is wrong with their child. Second, the child will usually feel less embarrassed when he finds out that other family members wet the bed.

Q *Why does bedwetting happen?*

A Bedwetting is due to a maturational delay in the way the brain and bladder communicate with each other at night. There are three main factors that contribute to the problem.

- **Bladder size:** Children who wet the bed usually have bladders that are smaller than their peers. This causes them to urinate more frequently during the day and their bladder has less room to "hold" urine at night.

- **Nighttime urine production:** The brain produces a hormone at night that reduces the amount of urine the kidneys make. Some children who wet the bed produce less of this hormone and thereby make more urine while they sleep.

- **"Deep" sleep:** Some children have difficulty waking up at night in response to internal or external stimuli. As a result, the brain may not respond when the bladder signals that the child needs to urinate.

Q *Do medical disorders cause bedwetting?*

A If your child has always been wet at night, a medical problem is unlikely to be the cause of his bedwetting. However, if she starts wetting after being dry for six months or more, a medical problem may be the cause. Such conditions can be readily identified by your child's doctor.

46

Q *Do food allergies cause bedwetting?*

A There is no research that proves a connection between food allergies and bedwetting. Some foods and beverages, such as chocolate, very salty foods, and drinks that contain caffeine, can make a child produce more urine. So it's a good idea to avoid these things at dinner.

Q *Does stress cause bedwetting?*

A Stressful situations like moving to a new home, changing schools, or the death of a loved one can trigger bedwetting. The wetting usually resolves when the stress passes. Emotional problems are not responsible for bedwetting in a child who has always had the problem.

Q *Does bedwetting go away on its own?*

A Every year, 15% of children who wet the bed become dry with no intervention. Although children usually follow the same pattern as their family members, this is not always the case.

Q *How do I know if my child is ready to do a bedwetting program?*

A Because there is no way to predict when a child will overcome his wetting, parents should consider a bedwetting program whenever the child appears motivated to become dry. Here are five signs to look for to see if a child is ready.

- He starts to notice that he's wet in the morning and doesn't like it.

- He tells you he doesn't want to wear Pull-Ups anymore.

- He tells you he wants to be dry at night.

- He asks if you wet the bed when you were a child.

- He doesn't want to go on sleepovers because he's wet at night.

Q *What can I do to help my child feel better about himself and bedwetting?*

A First and foremost, parents should never punish a child for being wet. Instead, parents should maintain a low-key attitude after wetting episodes. Parents can further help their child feel better by taking the following steps:

• Remind the child that bedwetting is no one's fault.

• Let the child know if anyone in the family wet the bed growing up.

• Make sure your child's siblings do not tease him about wetting the bed.

• Reinforce any efforts your child makes to help with his wetting, such as changing the sheets or helping you carry wet bedding to the laundry room.

• Praise your child for waking up at night to urinate, having smaller wet spots, or having a dry night.

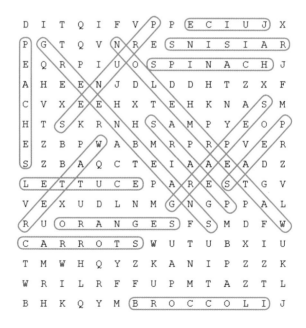

Answer key to page 44 Word Search.